Goethe

Iphigenia in Tauris

Goethe

Iphigenia in Tauris

1. Auflage | ISBN: 978-3-75236-332-6

Erscheinungsort: Frankfurt am Main, Deutschland

Erscheinungsjahr: 2020

Outlook Verlag GmbH, Deutschland.

Reproduktion des Originals.

GOETHE'S
Iphigenia In Tauris

ACT THE FIRST.

SCENE I.

A Grove before the Temple of Diana.

IPHIGENIA.

Beneath your leafy gloom, ye waving boughs
Of this old, shady, consecrated grove,
As in the goddess' silent sanctuary,
With the same shudd'ring feeling forth I step,
As when I trod it first, nor ever here
Doth my unquiet spirit feel at home.
Long as the mighty will, to which I bow,
Hath kept me here conceal'd, still, as at first,
I feel myself a stranger. For the sea
Doth sever me, alas! from those I love,
And day by day upon the shore I stand,
My soul still seeking for the land of Greece.
But to my sighs, the hollow-sounding waves
Bring, save their own hoarse murmurs, no reply.
Alas for him! who friendless and alone,
Remote from parents and from brethren dwells;
From him grief snatches every coming joy
Ere it doth reach his lip. His restless thoughts
Revert for ever to his father's halls,
Where first to him the radiant sun unclos'd
The gates of heav'n; where closer, day by day,
Brothers and sisters, leagu'd in pastime sweet,
Around each other twin'd the bonds of love.
I will not judge the counsel of the gods;

Yet, truly, woman's lot doth merit pity.
Man rules alike at home and in the field,
Nor is in foreign climes without resource;
Possession gladdens him, him conquest crowns,
And him an honourable death awaits.
How circumscrib'd is woman's destiny!
Obedience to a harsh, imperious lord,
Her duty, and her comfort; sad her fate,

2

Whom hostile fortune drives to lands remote:
Thus I, by noble Thoas, am detain'd,
Bound with a heavy, though a sacred chain.
Oh! with what shame, Diana, I confess
That with repugnance I perform these rites
For thee, divine protectress! unto whom
I would in freedom dedicate my life.
In thee, Diana, I have always hop'd,
And still I hope in thee, who didst infold
Within the holy shelter of thine arm
The outcast daughter of the mighty king.
Daughter of Jove! hast thou from ruin'd Troy
Led back in triumph to his native land
The mighty man, whom thou didst sore afflict,
His daughter's life in sacrifice demanding,—
Hast thou for him, the godlike Agamemnon,
Who to thine altar led his darling child,
Preserv'd his wife, Electra, and his son.
His dearest treasures?—then at length restore
Thy suppliant also to her friends and home,
And save her, as thou once from death didst save,
So now, from living here, a second death.

SCENE II.

IPHIGENIA.   ARKAS.

ARKAS.

The king hath sent me hither, and commands
To hail Diana's priestess. This the day,
On which for new and wonderful success,
Tauris her goddess thanks. The king and host
Draw near,—I come to herald their approach.

IPHIGENIA.

We are prepar'd to give them worthy greeting;
Our goddess doth behold with gracious eye
The welcome sacrifice from Thoas' hand.

ARKAS.

3

Oh, priestess, that thine eye more mildly beam'd,—
Thou much-rever'd one,—that I found thy glance,
O consecrated maid, more calm, more bright,
To all a happy omen! Still doth grief,
With gloom mysterious, shroud thy inner mind;
Still, still, through many a year we wait in vain
For one confiding utt'rance from thy breast.
Long as I've known thee in this holy place,
That look of thine hath ever made me shudder;
And, as with iron bands, thy soul remains
Lock'd in the deep recesses of thy breast.

IPHIGENIA.

As doth become the exile and the orphan.

ARKAS.

Dost thou then here seem exil'd and an orphan?

IPHIGENIA.

Can foreign scenes our fatherland replace?

ARKAS.

Thy fatherland is foreign now to thee.

IPHIGENIA.

Hence is it that my bleeding heart ne'er heals.
In early youth, when first my soul, in love,
Held father, mother, brethren fondly twin'd,
A group of tender germs, in union sweet,
We sprang in beauty from the parent stem,
And heavenward grew. An unrelenting curse
Then seiz'd and sever'd me from those I lov'd,
And wrench'd with iron grasp the beauteous bands.
It vanish'd then, the fairest charm of youth,
The simple gladness of life's early dawn;
Though sav'd, I was a shadow of myself,
And life's fresh joyance bloom'd in me no more.

ARKAS.

If thus thou ever dost lament thy fate,
I must accuse thee of ingratitude.

IPHIGENIA.

Thanks have you ever.

ARKAS.

Not the honest thanks
Which prompt the heart to offices of love;
The joyous glance, revealing to the host
A grateful spirit, with its lot content.
When thee a deep mysterious destiny
Brought to this sacred fane, long years ago.
To greet thee, as a treasure sent from heaven,
With reverence and affection, Thoas came.
Benign and friendly was this shore to thee,
Which had before each stranger's heart appall'd,
For, till thy coming, none e'er trod our realm
But fell, according to an ancient rite,
A bloody victim at Diana's shrine.

IPHIGENIA.

Freely to breathe alone is not to live.
Say, is it life, within this holy fane,
Like a poor ghost around its sepulchre
To linger out my days? Or call you that
A life of conscious happiness and joy,
When every hour, dream'd listlessly away,
Leads to those dark and melancholy days,
Which the sad troop of the departed spend
In self-forgetfulness on Lethe's shore?
A useless life is but an early death;
This, woman's lot, is eminently mine.

ARKAS.

I can forgive, though I must needs deplore,
The noble pride which underrates itself
It robs thee of the happiness of life.
And hast thou, since thy coming here, done nought?
Who cheer'd the gloomy temper of the king?
Who hath with gentle eloquence annull'd,
From year to year, the usage of our sires,
By which, a victim at Diana's shrine,
Each stranger perish'd, thus from certain death
Sending so oft the rescued captive home?
Hath not Diana, harbouring no revenge

5

For this suspension of her bloody rites,

In richest measure heard thy gentle prayer?
On joyous pinions o'er the advancing host,
Doth not triumphant conquest proudly soar?
And feels not every one a happier lot,
Since Thoas, who so long hath guided us
With wisdom and with valour, sway'd by thee,
The joy of mild benignity approves,
Which leads him to relax the rigid claims
Of mute submission? Call thyself useless! Thou,
Thou, from whose being o'er a thousand hearts,
A healing balsam flows? when to a race.
To whom a god consign'd thee, thou dost prove
A fountain of perpetual happiness,
And from this dire inhospitable shore
Dost to the stranger grant a safe return?

IPHIGENIA.

The little done doth vanish to the mind,
Which forward sees how much remains to do.

ARKAS.

Him dost thou praise, who underrates his deeds?

IPHIGENIA.

Who estimates his deeds is justly blam'd.

ARKAS.

We blame alike, who proudly disregard
Their genuine merit, and who vainly prize
Their spurious worth too highly. Trust me, priestess,
And hearken to the counsel of a man
With honest zeal devoted to thy service:
When Thoas comes to-day to speak with thee,
Lend to his purpos'd words a gracious ear.

IPHIGENIA.

The well-intention'd counsel troubles me:
His offer studiously I've sought to shun.

ARKAS.

Thy duty and thy interest calmly weigh.

Since the king lost his son, he trusts but few,
Nor those as formerly. Each noble's son
He views with jealous eye as his successor;
He dreads a solitary, helpless age,
Or rash rebellion, or untimely death.
A Scythian studies not the rules of speech,

And least of all the king. He who is used
To act and to command, knows not the art,
From far, with subtle tact, to guide discourse
Through many windings to its destin'd goal.
Do not embarrass him with shy reserve
And studied misconception: graciously,
And with submission, meet the royal wish.

IPHIGENIA.

Shall I then speed the doom that threatens me?

ARKAS.

His gracious offer canst thou call a threat?

IPHIGENIA.

'Tis the most terrible of all to me.

ARKAS.

For his affection grant him confidence.

IPHIGENIA.

If he will first redeem my soul from fear.

ARKAS.

Why dost thou hide from him thy origin?

IPHIGENIA.

A priestess secrecy doth well become.

ARKAS.

Nought to our monarch should a secret be;
And, though he doth not seek to fathom thine,
His noble nature feels, ay, deeply feels,
That studiously thou hid'st thyself from him.

IPHIGENIA.

Displeasure doth he harbour 'gainst me, then?

ARKAS.

Almost it seems so. True, he speaks not of thee.
But casual words have taught me that the wish
To call thee his hath firmly seiz'd his soul;
Oh, do not leave the monarch to himself!
Lest his displeasure, rip'ning in his breast,
Should work thee woe, so with repentance thou
Too late my faithful counsel shalt recall.

IPHIGENIA.

How! doth the monarch purpose what no man
Of noble mind, who loves his honest name,
Whose bosom reverence for the gods restrains,
Would ever think of? Will he force employ

To tear me from this consecrated fane?
Then will I call the gods, and chiefly thee,
Diana, goddess resolute, to aid me;
Thyself a virgin, thou'lt a virgin shield,
And succour to thy priestess gladly yield.

ARKAS.

Be tranquil! Passion, and youth's fiery blood
Impel not Thoas rashly to commit
A deed so lawless. In his present mood,
I fear from him another harsh resolve,
Which (for his soul is steadfast and unmov'd,)
He then will execute without delay.
Therefore I pray thee, canst thou grant no more,
At least be grateful—give thy confidence.

IPHIGENIA.

Oh tell me what is further known to thee.

ARKAS.

Learn it from him. I see the king approach;
Thou honour'st him, and thy own heart will prompt thee
To meet him kindly and with confidence.
A noble man by woman's gentle word
May oft be led.

IPHIGENIA, *alone.*

I see not how I can
Follow the counsel of my faithful friend.
But willingly the duty I perform
Of giving thanks for benefits receiv'd,
And much I wish that to the king my lips
With truth could utter what would please his ear.

SCENE III.

IPHIGENIA. THOAS.

IPHIGENIA.

Her royal gifts the goddess shower on thee!
Imparting conquest, wealth, and high renown,
Dominion, and the welfare of thy house,
With the fulfilment of each pious wish,
That thou, who over numbers rul'st supreme,
Thyself may'st be supreme in happiness!

THOAS.

Contented were I with my people's praise;
My conquests others more than I enjoy.
Oh! be he king or subject, he's most blest,
Who in his home finds happiness and peace.
Thou shar'dst my sorrow, when a hostile sword
Tore from my side my last, my dearest son;
Long as fierce vengeance occupied my heart,
I did not feel my dwelling's dreary void;
But now, returning home, my rage appeas'd,
My foes defeated, and my son aveng'd,
I find there nothing left to comfort me.
The glad obedience, which I used to see
Kindling in every eye, is smother'd now
In discontent and gloom; each, pond'ring, weighs
The changes which a future day may bring,
And serves the childless king, because compell'd.
To-day I come within this sacred fane,
Which I have often enter'd to implore
And thank the gods for conquest. In my breast
I bear an old and fondly-cherish'd wish.

To which methinks thou canst not be a stranger;
Thee, maid, a blessing to myself and realm,
I hope, as bride, to carry to my home.

IPHIGENIA.

Too great thine offer, king, to one unknown;
Abash'd the fugitive before thee stands,
Who on this shore sought only what thou gav'st,
Safety and peace.

THOAS.

                    Thus still to shroud thyself
From me, as from the lowest, in the veil
Of mystery which wrapp'd thy coming here,
Would in no country be deem'd just or right.
Strangers this shore appall'd; 'twas so ordain'd
Alike by law and stern necessity.
From thee alone—a kindly welcom'd guest,
Who hast enjoy'd each hallow'd privilege,
And spent thy days in freedom unrestrain'd—
From thee I hop'd that confidence to gain
Which every faithful host may justly claim.

IPHIGENIA.

If I conceal'd, O king, my name, my race,
'Twas fear that prompted me, and not mistrust.
For didst thou know who stands before thee now,
And what accursed head thy arm protects,
A shudd'ring horror would possess thy heart;
And, far from wishing me to share thy throne,
Thou, ere the time appointed, from thy realm
Wouldst banish me perchance, and thrust me forth,
Before a glad reunion with my friends
And period to my wand'rings is ordain'd,
To meet that sorrow, which in every clime,
With cold, inhospitable, fearful hand,
Awaits the outcast, exil'd from his home.

THOAS.

Whate'er respecting thee the gods decree,
Whate'er their doom for thee and for thy house,
Since thou hast dwelt amongst us, and enjoy'd

10

The privilege the pious stranger claims,
To me hath fail'd no blessing sent from Heaven;
And to persuade me, that protecting thee
I shield a guilty head, were hard indeed.

IPHIGENIA.

Thy bounty, not the guest, draws blessings down.

THOAS.

The kindness shown the wicked is not blest.
End then thy silence, priestess; not unjust
Is he who doth demand it. In my hands
The goddess plac'd thee; thou hast been to me
As sacred as to her, and her behest
Shall for the future also be my law.
If thou canst hope in safety to return
Back to thy kindred, I renounce my claims:
But is thy homeward path for ever clos'd—
Or doth thy race in hopeless exile rove,
Or lie extinguish'd by some mighty woe—
Then may I claim thee by more laws than one.
Speak openly, thou know'st I keep my word.

IPHIGENIA.

Its ancient bands reluctantly my tongue
Doth loose, a long-hid secret to divulge;

For once imparted, it resumes no more
The safe asylum of the inmost heart,
But thenceforth, as the powers above decree,
Doth work its ministry of weal or woe.
Attend! I issue from the Titan's race.

THOAS.

A word momentous calmly hast thou spoken.
Him nam'st thou ancestor whom all the world
Knows as a sometime favourite of the gods?
Is it that Tantalus, whom Jove himself
Drew to his council and his social board?
On whose experienc'd words, with wisdom fraught,
As on the language of an oracle,
E'en gods delighted hung?

IPHIGENIA.

'Tis even he;
But gods should not hold intercourse with men
As with themselves. Too weak the human race,
Not to grow dizzy on unwonted heights.
Ignoble was he not, and no betrayer;
To be the Thunderer's slave, he was too great:
To be his friend and comrade,—but a man.
His crime was human, and their doom severe;
For poets sing, that treachery and pride
Did from Jove's table hurl him headlong down,
To grovel in the depths of Tartarus.
Alas, and his whole race their hate pursues.

THOAS.

Bear they their own guilt, or their ancestors'?

IPHIGENIA.

The Titan's mighty breast and nervous frame
Was his descendant's certain heritage;
But round their brow Jove forg'd a band of brass.
Wisdom and patience, prudence and restraint,
He from their gloomy, fearful eye conceal'd;
In them each passion grew to savage rage,
And headlong rush'd uncheck'd. The Titan's son,
The strong-will'd Pelops, won his beauteous bride,
Hippodamia, child of Œnomaus,
Through treachery and murder; she ere long
Bore him two children, Atreus and Thyestes;

With envy they beheld the growing love
Their father cherish'd for a first-born son
Sprung from another union. Bound by hate,
In secret they contrive their brother's death.
The sire, the crime imputing to his wife,
With savage fury claim'd from her his child,
And she in terror did destroy herself—

THOAS.

Thou'rt silent? Pause not in thy narrative!
Do not repent thy confidence—say on!

IPHIGENIA.

How blest is he who his progenitors
With pride remembers, to the list'ner tells
The story of their greatness, of their deeds,
And, silently rejoicing, sees himself
Link'd to this goodly chain! For the same stock
Bears not the monster and the demigod:
A line, or good or evil, ushers in
The glory or the terror of the world.—
After the death of Pelops, his two sons
Rul'd o'er the city with divided sway.
But such an union could not long endure.
His brother's honour first Thyestes wounds.
In vengeance Atreus drove him from the realm.
Thyestes, planning horrors, long before
Had stealthily procur'd his brother's son,
Whom he in secret nurtur'd as his own.
Revenge and fury in his breast he pour'd,
Then to the royal city sent him forth,
That in his uncle he might slay his sire,
The meditated murder was disclos'd,
And by the king most cruelly aveng'd,
Who slaughter'd, as he thought, his brother's son.
Too late he learn'd whose dying tortures met
His drunken gaze; and seeking to assuage
The insatiate vengeance that possess'd his soul,
He plann'd a deed unheard of. He assum'd
A friendly tone, seem'd reconcil'd, appeas'd.
And lur'd his brother, with his children twain,
Back to his kingdom; these he seiz'd and slew;
Then plac'd the loathsome and abhorrent food

At his first meal before the unconscious sire.
And when Thyestes had his hunger still'd
With his own flesh, a sadness seiz'd his soul;
He for his children ask'd,—their steps, their voice,
Fancied he heard already at the door;
And Atreus, grinning with malicious joy,
Threw in the members of the slaughter'd boys.—
Shudd'ring, O king, thou dost avert thy face:
So did the sun his radiant visage hide,
And swerve his chariot from the eternal path.
These, monarch, are thy priestess' ancestors,

13

And many a dreadful fate of mortal doom,
And many a deed of the bewilder'd brain,
Dark night doth cover with her sable wing,
Or shroud in gloomy twilight.

THOAS.

Hidden there
Let them abide. A truce to horror now,
And tell me by what miracle thou sprang'st
From race so savage.

IPHIGENIA.

Atreus' eldest son
Was Agamemnon; he, O king, my sire:
But I may say with truth, that, from a child,
In him the model of a perfect man
I witness'd ever. Clytemnestra bore
To him, myself, the firstling of their love,
Electra then. Peaceful the monarch rul'd,
And to the house of Tantalus was given
A long-withheld repose. A son alone
Was wanting to complete my parent's bliss;
Scarce was this wish fulfill'd, and young Orestes,
The household's darling, with his sisters grew,
When new misfortunes vex'd our ancient house.
To you hath come the rumour of the war,
Which, to avenge the fairest woman's wrongs,
The force united of the Grecian kings
Round Ilion's walls encamp'd. Whether the town
Was humbl'd, and achiev'd their great revenge
I have not heard. My father led the host
In Aulis vainly for a favouring gale

They waited; for, enrag'd against their chief,
Diana stay'd their progress, and requir'd,
Through Calchas' voice, the monarch's eldest daughter.
They lur'd me with my mother to the camp,
And at Diana's altar doom'd this head.—
She was appeas'd, she did not wish my blood,
And wrapt me in a soft protecting cloud;
Within this temple from the dream of death
I waken'd first. Yes, I myself am she;
Iphigenia,—I who speak to thee

14

Am Atreus' grandchild, Agamemnon's child,
And great Diana's consecrated priestess.

THOAS.

I yield no higher honour or regard
To the king's daughter than the maid unknown;
Once more my first proposal I repeat;
Come, follow me, and share what I possess.

IPHIGENIA.

How dare I venture such a step, O king?
Hath not the goddess who protected me
Alone a right to my devoted head?
'Twas she who chose for me this sanctuary,
Where she perchance reserves me for my sire,
By my apparent death enough chastis'd,
To be the joy and solace of his age.
Perchance my glad return is near; and how
If I, unmindful of her purposes,
Had here attach'd myself against her will?
I ask'd a signal, did she wish my stay.

THOAS.

The signal is that still thou tarriest here.
Seek not evasively such vain pretexts.
Not many words are needed to refuse,
By the refus'd the *no* alone is heard.

IPHIGENIA.

Mine are not words meant only to deceive;
I have to thee my inmost heart reveal'd.
And doth no inward voice suggest to thee,
How I with yearning soul must pine to see
My father, mother, and my long-lost home?

Oh let thy vessels bear me thither, king!
That in the ancient halls, where sorrow still
In accents low doth fondly breathe my name,
Joy, as in welcome of a new-born child,
May round the columns twine the fairest wreath.
Thou wouldst to me and mine new life impart.

THOAS.

Then go! the promptings of thy heart obey;
Despise the voice of reason and good counsel.
Be quite the woman, sway'd by each desire,
That bridleless impels her to and fro.
When passion rages fiercely in her breast,
No sacred tie withholds her from the wretch
Who would allure her to forsake for him
A husband's or a father's guardian arms;
Extinct within her heart its fiery glow,
The golden tongue of eloquence in vain
With words of truth and power assails her ear.

IPHIGENIA.

Remember now, O king, thy noble words!
My trust and candour wilt thou thus repay?
Thou seem'dst, methought, prepar'd to hear the truth.

THOAS.

For this unlook'd-for answer not prepar'd.
Yet 'twas to be expected; knew I not
That 'twas with woman I had now to deal?

IPHIGENIA.

Upbraid not thus, O king, our feeble sex!
Though not in dignity to match with yours,
The weapons woman wields are not ignoble.
And trust me, Thoas, in thy happiness
I have a deeper insight than thyself.
Thou thinkest, ignorant alike of both,
A closer union would augment our bliss;
Inspir'd with confidence and honest zeal
Thou strongly urgest me to yield consent;
And here I thank the gods, who give me strength
To shun a doom unratified by them.

THOAS.

'Tis not a god, 'tis thine own heart that speaks.

IPHIGENIA.

'Tis through the heart alone they speak to us.

THOAS.

To hear them have I not an equal right?

IPHIGENIA.

The raging tempest drowns the still, small voice.

THOAS.

This voice no doubt the priestess hears alone.

IPHIGENIA.

Before all others should the prince attend it.

THOAS.

Thy sacred office, and ancestral right
To Jove's own table, place thee with the gods
In closer union than an earth-born savage.

IPHIGENIA.

Thus must I now the confidence atone
Thyself extorted from me!

THOAS.

                         I'm a man,
And better 'tis we end this conference.
Hear then my last resolve. Be priestess still
Of the great goddess who selected thee;
And may she pardon me, that I from her,
Unjustly and with secret self-reproach,
Her ancient sacrifice so long withheld.
From olden times no stranger near'd our shore
But fell a victim at her sacred shrine.
But thou, with kind affection (which at times
Seem'd like a gentle daughter's tender love,
At times assum'd to my enraptur'd heart
The modest inclination of a bride),
Didst so inthral me, as with magic bonds,
That I forgot my duty. Thou didst rock
My senses in a dream: I did not hear
My people's murmurs: now they cry aloud,
Ascribing my poor son's untimely death
To this my guilt. No longer for thy sake
Will I oppose the wishes of the crowd,
Who urgently demand the sacrifice.

IPHIGENIA.

For mine own sake I ne'er desired it from thee.

Who to the gods ascribe a thirst for blood
Do misconceive their nature, and impute
To them their own inhuman dark desires.
Did not Diana snatch me from the priest,
Preferring my poor service to my death?

THOAS.

'Tis not for us, on reason's shifting grounds,
Lightly to guide and construe rites divine.
Perform thy duty; I'll accomplish mine.
Two strangers, whom in caverns of the shore
We found conceal'd, and whose arrival here
Bodes to my realm no good, are in my power.
With them thy goddess may once more resume
Her ancient, pious, long-suspended rites!
I send them here,—thy duty not unknown.   [*Exit.*

IPHIGENIA, *alone.*

Gracious protectress! thou hast clouds
To shelter innocence distress'd,
And genial gales from Fate's rude grasp,
Safely to waft her o'er the sea,
O'er the wide earth's remotest realms,
Where'er it seemeth good to thee.
Wise art thou,—thine all-seeing eye
The future and the past surveys,
And doth on all thy children rest,
E'en as thy pure and guardian light
Keeps o'er the earth its silent watch,
The beauty and the life of night.
O Goddess! keep my hands from blood!
Blessing it never brings, nor peace;
And still in evil hours the form
Of the chance-murder'd man appears
To fill the unwilling murderer's soul
With horrible and gloomy fears.
For fondly the Immortals view
Man's widely-scatter'd, simple race;
And the poor mortal's transient life
Gladly prolong, that he may raise
Awhile to their eternal heavens

His sympathetic joyous gaze.

ACT THE SECOND.

SCENE I.

ORESTES.   PYLADES.

ORESTES.

It is the path of death that now we tread:
At every step my soul grows more serene.
When I implor'd Apollo to remove
The grisly band of Furies from my side,
He seem'd, with hope-inspiring, godlike words,
To promise aid and safety in the fane
Of his lov'd sister, who o'er Tauris rules.
Thus the prophetic word fulfils itself,
That with my life shall terminate my woe.
How easy 'tis for me, whose heart is crush'd,
Whose sense is deaden'd by a hand divine,
Thus to renounce the beauteous light of day!
And must the son of Atreus not entwine
The wreath of conquest round his dying brow—
Must I, as my forefathers, as my sire,
Bleed like a victim,—an ignoble death—
So be it! Better at the altar here,
Than in a nook obscure, where kindred hands
Have spread assassination's wily net.
Yield me this brief repose, infernal Powers!
Ye, who, like loosen'd hounds, still scent the blood,
Which, trickling from my feet, betrays my path.
Leave me! ere long I come to you below.
Nor you, nor I, should view the light of day.
The soft green carpet of the beauteous earth
Is no arena for unhallow'd fiends.
Below I seek you, where an equal fate
Binds all in murky, never-ending night.
Thee only, thee, my Pylades, my friend,
The guiltless partner of my crime and curse,
Thee am I loath, before thy time, to take

20

To yonder cheerless shore! Thy life or death
Alone awakens in me hope or fear.

PYLADES.

Like thee, Orestes, I am not prepar'd
Downwards to wander to yon realm of shade.
I purpose still, through the entangl'd paths,
Which seem as they would lead to blackest night,
Again to guide our upward way to life.
Of death I think not; I observe and mark
Whether the gods may not perchance present
Means and fit moment for a joyful flight.
Dreaded or not, the stroke of death must come;
And though the priestess stood with hand uprais'd,
Prepar'd to cut our consecrated locks,
Our safety still should be my only thought:
Uplift thy soul above this weak despair;
Desponding doubts but hasten on our peril.
Apollo pledg'd to us his sacred word,
That in his sister's holy fane for thee
Were comfort, aid, and glad return prepar'd.
The words of Heaven are not equivocal,
As in despair the poor oppress'd one thinks.

ORESTES.

The mystic web of life my mother spread
Around my infant head, and so I grew,
An image of my sire; and my mute look
Was aye a bitter and a keen reproof
To her and base Ægisthus. Oh, how oft,
When silently within our gloomy hall
Electra sat, and mus'd beside the fire,
Have I with anguish'd spirit climb'd her knee,
And watch'd her bitter tears with sad amaze!
Then would she tell me of our noble sire:
How much I long'd to see him—be with him!
Myself at Troy one moment fondly wish'd,
My sire's return, the next. The day arrived—

PYLADES.

Oh, of that awful hour let fiends of hell
Hold nightly converse! Of a time more fair
May the remembrance animate our hearts
To fresh heroic deeds. The gods require
On this wide earth the service of the good,

To work their pleasure. Still they count on thee;

For in thy father's train they sent thee not,
When he to Orcus went unwilling down.

ORESTES.

Would I had seiz'd the border of his robe.
And follow'd him!

PYLADES.

       They kindly car'd for me
Who here detain'd thee; for if thou hadst died
I know not what had then become of me;
Since I with thee, and for thy sake alone,
Have from my childhood liv'd, and wish to live.

ORESTES.

Do not remind me of those tranquil days,
When me thy home a safe asylum gave;
With fond solicitude thy noble sire
The half-nipp'd, tender flow'ret gently rear'd;
While thou a friend and playmate always gay,
Like to a light and brilliant butterfly
Around a dusky flower, didst around me
Still with new life thy merry gambols play,
And breathe thy joyous spirit in my soul,
Until, my cares forgetting, I with thee
Was lur'd to snatch the eager joys of youth.

PYLADES.

My very life began when thee I lov'd.

ORESTES.

Say, then thy woes began, and thou speak'st truly.
This is the sharpest sorrow of my lot,
That, like a plague-infected wretch, I bear
Death and destruction hid within my breast;
That, where I tread, e'en on the healthiest spot,
Ere long the blooming faces round betray
The writhing features of a ling'ring death.

PYLADES.

Were thy breath venom, I had been the first
To die that death, Orestes. Am I not,
As ever, full of courage and of joy?

23

And love and courage are the spirit's wings
Wafting to noble actions.

ORESTES.

                        Noble actions?
Time was, when fancy painted such before us!
When oft, the game pursuing, on we roam'd
O'er hill and valley; hoping that ere long
With club and weapon arm'd, we so might track
The robber to his den, or monster huge.
And then at twilight, by the glassy sea,
We peaceful sat, reclin'd against each other
The waves came dancing to our very feet.
And all before us lay the wide, wide world.
Then on a sudden one would seize his sword,
And future deeds shone round us like the stars,
Which gemm'd in countless throngs the vault of night.

PYLADES.

Endless, my friend, the projects which the soul
Burns to accomplish. We would every deed
At once perform as grandly as it shows
After long ages, when from land to land
The poet's swelling song hath roll'd it on.
It sounds so lovely what our fathers did,
When, in the silent evening shade reclin'd,
We drink it in with music's melting tones;
And what we do is, as their deeds to them,
Toilsome and incomplete!
Thus we pursue what always flies before;
We disregard the path in which we tread,
Scarce see around the footsteps of our sires,
Or heed the trace of their career on earth.
We ever hasten on to chase their shades,
Which godlike, at a distance far remote,
On golden clouds reclin'd, the mountains crown.
The man I prize not who esteems himself
Just as the people's breath may chance to raise him.
But thou, Orestes, to the gods give thanks,
That they have done so much through thee already.

ORESTES.

When they ordain a man to noble deeds,
To shield from dire calamity his friends,
Extend his empire, or protect its bounds,
Or put to flight its ancient enemies,

Let him be grateful! For to him a god
Imparts the first, the sweetest joy of life.
Me have they doom'd to be a slaughterer,
To be an honour'd mother's murderer,
And shamefully a deed of shame avenging.
Me through their own decree they have o'erwhelm'd.
Trust me, the race of Tantalus is doom'd;
Nor may his last descendant leave the earth,
Or crown'd with honour or unstain'd by crime.

PYLADES.

The gods avenge not on the son the deeds
Done by the father. Each, or good or bad,
Of his own actions reaps the due reward.
The parents' blessing, not their curse, descends.

ORESTES.

Methinks their blessing did not lead us here.

PYLADES.

It was at least the mighty gods' decree.

ORESTES.

Then is it their decree which doth destroy us.

PYLADES.

Perform what they command, and wait the event.
Do thou Apollo's sister bear from hence,
That they at Delphi may united dwell,
Rever'd and honour'd by a noble race:
Thee, for this deed, the heav'nly pair will view
With gracious eye, and from the hateful grasp
Of the infernal Powers will rescue thee.
E'en now none dares intrude within this grove.

ORESTES.

So shall I die at least a peaceful death.

PYLADES.

25

Far other are my thoughts, and not unskill'd
Have I the future and the past combin'd
In quiet meditation. Long, perchance,
Hath ripen'd in the counsel of the gods
The great event. Diana wish'd to leave
This savage region foul with human blood.
We were selected for the high emprize;
To us it is assign'd, and strangely thus
We are conducted to the threshold here.

ORESTES.

My friend, with wondrous skill thou link'st thy wish
With the predestin'd purpose of the gods.

PYLADES.

Of what avail is prudence, if it fail
Heedful to mark the purposes of Heaven?
A noble man, who much hath sinn'd, some god
Doth summon to a dangerous enterprize,
Which to achieve appears impossible.
The hero conquers, and atoning serves
Mortals and gods, who thenceforth honour him.

ORESTES.

Am I foredoom'd to action and to life,
Would that a god from my distemper'd brain
Might chase this dizzy fever, which impels
My restless steps along a slipp'ry path,
Stain'd with a mother's blood, to direful death;
And pitying, dry the fountain, whence the blood,
For ever spouting from a mother's wounds,
Eternally defiles me!

PYLADES.

          Wait in peace!
Thou dost increase the evil, and dost take
The office of the Furies on thyself.
Let me contrive,—be still! And when at length
The time for action claims our powers combin'd,
Then will I summon thee, and on we'll stride,
With cautious boldness to achieve the event.

ORESTES.

I hear Ulysses speak!

PYLADES.

Nay, mock me not.
Each must select the hero after whom
To climb the steep and difficult ascent
Of high Olympus. And to me it seems
That him nor stratagem nor art defile
Who consecrates himself to noble deeds.

ORESTES.

I most esteem the brave and upright man.

PYLADES.

And therefore have I not desir'd thy counsel.
One step is ta'en already: from our guards
I have extorted this intelligence.
A strange and godlike woman now restrains
The execution of that bloody law:
Incense, and prayer, and an unsullied heart,
These are the gifts she offers to the gods.
Her fame is widely spread, and it is thought
That from the race of Amazon she springs,
And hither fled some great calamity.

ORESTES.

Her gentle sway, it seems, lost all its power
At the approach of one so criminal,
Whom the dire curse enshrouds in gloomy night.
Our doom to seal, the pious thirst for blood
Again unchains the ancient cruel rite:
The monarch's savage will decrees our death;
A woman cannot save when he condemns.

PYLADES.

That 'tis a woman is a ground for hope!
A man, the very best, with cruelty
At length may so familiarize his mind,
His character through custom so transform,
That he shall come to make himself a law
Of what at first his very soul abhorr'd.
But woman doth retain the stamp of mind

She first assum'd. On her we may depend
In good or evil with more certainty.
She comes; leave us alone. I dare not tell
At once our names, nor unreserv'd confide
Our fortunes to her. Now retire awhile,
And ere she speaks with thee we'll meet again.

SCENE II.

IPHIGENIA.   PYLADES.

IPHIGENIA.

Whence art thou? Stranger, speak! To me thy bearing
Stamps thee of Grecian, not of Scythian race.

(She unbinds his chains.)

The freedom that I give is dangerous:
The gods avert the doom that threatens you!

PYLADES.

Delicious music! dearly welcome tones
Of our own language in a foreign land!
With joy my captive eye once more beholds
The azure mountains of my native coast.
Oh, let this joy that I too am a Greek
Convince thee, priestess! How I need thine aid,
A moment I forget, my spirit wrapt
In contemplation of so fair a vision.
If fate's dread mandate doth not seal thy lips.
From which of our illustrious races, say,
Dost thou thy godlike origin derive?

IPHIGENIA.

A priestess, by the Goddess' self ordain'd
And consecrated too, doth speak with thee.
Let that suffice: but tell me, who art thou,
And what unbless'd o'erruling destiny
Hath hither led thee with thy friend?

PYLADES.

The woe,

Whose hateful presence ever dogs our steps,
I can with ease relate. Oh, would that thou
Couldst with like ease, divine one, shed on us
One ray of cheering hope! We are from Crete,
Adrastus' sons, and I, the youngest born,
Named Cephalus; my eldest brother, he,
Laodamus. Between us two a youth
Of savage temper grew, who oft disturb'd
The joy and concord of our youthful sports.
Long as our father led his powers at Troy,

Passive our mother's mandate we obey'd;
But when, enrich'd with booty, he return'd,
And shortly after died, a contest fierce
For the succession and their father's wealth,
Parted the brothers. I the eldest joined;
He slew the second; and the Furies hence
For kindred murder dog his restless steps.
But to this savage shore the Delphian god
Hath sent us, cheer'd by hope, commanding us
Within his sister's temple to await
The blessed hand of aid. We have been ta'en,
Brought hither, and now stand for sacrifice.
My tale is told.

IPHIGENIA.

Tell me, is Troy o'erthrown?
Assure me of its fall.

PYLADES.

It lies in ruins.
But oh, ensure deliverance to us!
Hasten, I pray, the promis'd aid of heav'n.
Pity my brother, say a kindly word;
But I implore thee, spare him when thou speakest.
Too easily his inner mind is torn
By joy, or grief, or cruel memory.
A feverish madness oft doth seize on him,
Yielding his spirit, beautiful and free,
A prey to furies.

IPHIGENIA.

Great as is thy woe,

29

Forget it, I conjure thee, for awhile,
Till I am satisfied.

PYLADES.

               The stately town,
Which ten long years withstood the Grecian host,
Now lies in ruins, ne'er to rise again;
Yet many a hero's grave will oft recall
Our sad remembrance to that barbarous shore;
There lies Achilles and his noble friend.

IPHIGENIA.

And are ye, godlike forms, reduc'd to dust!

PYLADES.

Nor Palamede, nor Ajax, ere again
The daylight of their native land behold.

IPHIGENIA.

He speaks not of my father, doth not name
Him with the fallen. He may yet survive!
I may behold him! still hope on, my heart!

PYLADES.

Yet happy are the thousands who receiv'd
Their bitter death-blow from a hostile hand!
For terror wild, and end most tragical,
Some hostile, angry, deity prepar'd,
Instead of triumph, for the home-returning.
Do human voices never reach this shore?
Far as their sound extends, they bear the fame
Of deeds unparallel'd. And is the woe
Which fills Mycene's halls with ceaseless sighs
To thee a secret still?—And know'st thou not
That Clytemnestra, with Ægisthus' aid,
Her royal consort artfully ensnar'd,
And murder'd on the day of his return?—
The monarch's house thou honourest! I perceive
Thy heaving bosom vainly doth contend
With tidings fraught with such unlook'd-for woe
Art thou the daughter of a friend? or born
Within the circuit of Mycene's walls?

Do not conceal it, nor avenge on me
That here the horrid crime I first announc'd.

IPHIGENIA.

Proceed, and tell me how the deed was done.

PYLADES.

The day of his return, as from the bath
Arose the monarch, tranquil and refresh'd.
His robe demanding from his consort's hand,
A tangl'd garment, complicate with folds.
She o'er his shoulders flung and noble head;
And when, as from a net, he vainly strove
To extricate himself, the traitor, base
Ægisthus, smote him, and envelop'd thus
Great Agamemnon sought the shades below.

IPHIGENIA.

And what reward receiv'd the base accomplice?

PYLADES.

A queen and kingdom he possess'd already.

IPHIGENIA.

Base passion prompted, then, the deed of shame?

PYLADES.

And feelings, cherish'd long, of deep revenge.

IPHIGENIA.

How had the monarch injured Clytemnestra?

PYLADES.

By such a dreadful deed, that if on earth
Aught could exculpate murder, it were this.
To Aulis he allur'd her, when the fleet
With unpropitious winds the goddess stay'd;
And there, a victim at Diana's shrine,
The monarch, for the welfare of the Greeks,
Her eldest daughter doom'd. And this, 'tis said,
Planted such deep abhorrence in her heart,
That to Ægisthus she resign'd herself,
And round her husband flung the web of death.

31

IPHIGENIA (*veiling herself*).

It is enough! Thou wilt again behold me.

PYLADES, *alone*.

The fortune of this royal house, it seems,
Doth move her deeply. Whosoe'er she be,
She must herself have known the monarch well;—
For our good fortune, from a noble house,
She hath been sold to bondage. Peace, my heart!
And let us steer our course with prudent zeal
Toward the star of hope which gleams upon us.

ACT THE THIRD.

SCENE I.

IPHIGENIA.   ORESTES.

IPHIGENIA.

Unhappy man, I only loose thy bonds
In token of a still severer doom.
The freedom which the sanctuary imparts,

Like the last life-gleam o'er the dying face,
But heralds death. I cannot, dare not say
Your doom is hopeless; for, with murd'rous hand,
Could I inflict the fatal blow myself?
And while I here am priestess of Diana,
None, be he who he may, dare touch your heads.
But the incensed king, should I refuse
Compliance with the rites himself enjoin'd,
Will choose another virgin from my train
As my successor. Then, alas! with nought,
Save ardent wishes, can I succour you,
Much honour'd countryman! The humblest slave,
Who had but near'd our sacred household hearth,
Is dearly welcome in a foreign land;
How with proportion'd joy and blessing, then,
Shall I receive the man who doth recall
The image of the heroes, whom I learn'd
To honour from my parents, and who cheers
My inmost heart with flatt'ring gleams of hope!

ORESTES.

Does prudent forethought prompt thee to conceal
Thy name and race? or may I hope to know
Who, like a heavenly vision, meets me thus?

IPHIGENIA.

Yes, thou shalt know me. Now conclude the tale
Of which thy brother only told me half:

33

Relate their end, who coming home from Troy,
On their own threshold met a doom severe
And most unlook'd for. I, though but a child
When first conducted hither, well recall
The timid glance of wonder which I cast
On those heroic forms. When they went forth,
it seem'd as though Olympus from her womb
Had cast the heroes of a by-gone world,
To frighten Ilion; and, above them all,
Great Agamemnon tower'd pre-eminent!
Oh tell me! Fell the hero in his home,
Though Clytemnestra's and Ægisthus' wiles?

ORESTES.

He fell!

IPHIGENIA.

    Unblest Mycene! Thus the sons
Of Tantalus, with barbarous hands, have sown
Curse upon curse; and, as the shaken weed
Scatters around a thousand poison-seeds,
So they assassins ceaseless generate,
Their children's children ruthless to destroy.—
Now tell the remnant of thy brother's tale,
Which horror darkly hid from me before.
How did the last descendant of the race,—
The gentle child, to whom the Gods assign'd
The office of avenger,—how did he
Escape that day of blood? Did equal fate
Around Orestes throw Avernus' net?
Say, was he saved? and is he still alive?
And lives Electra, too?

ORESTES.

They both survive.

IPHIGENIA.

Golden Apollo, lend thy choicest beams!
Lay them an offering at the throne of Jove!
For I am poor and dumb.

ORESTES.

If social bonds
Or ties more close connect thee with this house,
As this thy joy evinces, rein thy heart;
For insupportable the sudden plunge
From happiness to sorrow's gloomy depth.
As yet thou only know'st the hero's death.

IPHIGENIA.

And is not this intelligence enough?

ORESTES.

Half of the horror yet remains untold.

IPHIGENIA.

Electra and Orestes both survive,
What have I then to fear?

ORESTES.

And fear'st thou nought
For Clytemnestra?

IPHIGENIA.

Her, nor hope nor fear
Have power to save.

ORESTES.

She to the land of hope
Hath bid farewell.

IPHIGENIA.

Did her repentant hand
Shed her own blood?

ORESTES.

Not so; yet her own blood
Inflicted death.

IPHIGENIA.

Speak less ambiguously.
Uncertainty around my anxious head
Her dusky, thousand-folded, pinion waves.

ORESTES.

Have then the powers above selected me
To be the herald of a dreadful deed,
Which, in the drear and soundless realms of night,
I fain would hide for ever? 'Gainst my will
Thy gentle voice constrains me; it demands,
And shall receive, a tale of direst woe.
Electra, on the day when fell her sire,
Her brother from impending doom conceal'd;
Him Strophius, his father's relative,
With kindest care receiv'd, and rear'd the child
With his own son, named Pylades, who soon
Around the stranger twin'd the bonds of love.
And as they grew, within their inmost souls
There sprang the burning longing to revenge
The monarch's death. Unlook'd for, and disguis'd,
They reach Mycene, feigning to have brought
The mournful tidings of Orestes' death,
Together with his ashes. Them the queen
Gladly receives. Within the house they enter;
Orestes to Electra shows himself:
She fans the fires of vengeance into flame,
Which in the sacred presence of a mother
Had burn'd more dimly. Silently she leads
Her brother to the spot where fell their sire;

Where lurid blood-marks, on the oft-wash'd floor,
With pallid streaks, anticipate revenge.
With fiery eloquence she pictures forth
Each circumstance of that atrocious deed,—
Her own oppress'd and miserable life,
The prosperous traitor's insolent demeanour,
The perils threat'ning Agamemnon's race
From her who had become their stepmother;
Then in his hand the ancient dagger thrusts,
Which often in the house of Tantalus
With savage fury rag'd,—and by her son
Is Clytemnestra slain.

IPHIGENIA.

Immortal powers!
Whose pure and blest existence glides away
'Mid ever shifting clouds, me have ye kept

36

So many years secluded from the world,
Retain'd me near yourselves, consign'd to me
The childlike task to feed the sacred fire,
And taught my spirit, like the hallow'd flame,
With never-clouded brightness to aspire
To your pure mansions,—but at length to feel
With keener woe the misery of my house?
Oh tell me of the poor unfortunate!
Speak of Orestes!

ORESTES.

Would that he were dead!
Forth from his mother's blood her ghost arose,
And to the ancient daughters of the night
Cries,—"Let him not escape,—the matricide!
Pursue the victim, dedicate to you!"
They hear, and glare around with hollow eyes,
Like greedy eagles. In their murky dens
They stir themselves, and from the corners creep
Their comrades, dire Remorse and pallid Fear;
Before them fumes a mist of Acheron;
Perplexingly around the murderer's brow
The eternal contemplation of the past
Rolls in its cloudy circles. Once again
The grisly band, commissioned to destroy,
Pollute earth's beautiful and heaven-sown fields,

From which an ancient curse had banish'd them.
Their rapid feet the fugitive pursue;
They only pause to start a wilder fear.

IPHIGENIA.

Unhappy one; thy lot resembles his,
Thou feel'st what he, poor fugitive, must suffer.

ORESTES.

What say'st thou? why presume my fate like his?

IPHIGENIA.

A brother's murder weighs upon thy soul;
Thy younger brother told the mournful tale.

ORESTES.

I cannot suffer that thy noble soul
Should be deceiv'd by error. Rich in guile,
And practis'd in deceit, a stranger may
A web of falsehood cunningly devise
To snare a stranger;—between us be truth.
I am Orestes! and this guilty head
Is stooping to the tomb, and covets death;
It will be welcome now in any shape.
Whoe'er thou art, for thee and for my friend
I wish deliverance;—I desire it not.
Thou seem'st to linger here against thy will;
Contrive some means of flight, and leave me here:
My lifeless corpse hurl'd headlong from the rock,
My blood shall mingle with the dashing waves,
And bring a curse upon this barbarous shore!
Return together home to lovely Greece,
With joy a new existence to commence.

[ORESTES *retires.*

IPHIGENIA.

At length Fulfilment, fairest child of Jove,
Thou dost descend upon me from on high!
How vast thine image! scarce my straining eye
Can reach thy hands, which, fill'd with golden fruit
And wreaths of blessing, from Olympus' height
Shower treasures down. As by his bounteous gifts
We recognize the monarch (for what seems
To thousands opulence is nought to him),
So you, ye heavenly Powers, are also known
By bounty long withheld, and wisely plann'd.

Ye only know what things are good for us;
Ye view the future's wide-extended realm;
While from our eye a dim or starry veil
The prospect shrouds. Calmly ye hear our prayers,
When we like children sue for greater speed.
Not immature ye pluck heaven's golden fruit;
And woe to him, who with impatient hand,
His date of joy forestalling, gathers death.
Let not this long-awaited happiness,
Which yet my heart hath scarcely realiz'd,
Like to the shadow of departed friends,

Glide vainly by with triple sorrow fraught!

ORESTES, *returning*.

Dost thou for Pylades and for thyself
Implore the gods, blend not my name with yours;
Thou wilt not save the wretch whom thou wouldst join,
But wilt participate his curse and woe.

IPHIGENIA.

My destiny is firmly bound to thine.

ORESTES.

No, say not so; alone and unattended
Let me descend to Hades. Though thou shouldst
In thine own veil enwrap the guilty one,
Thou couldst not shroud him from his wakeful foes;
And e'en thy sacred presence, heavenly maid,
Drives them aside, but scares them not away.
With brazen impious feet they dare not tread
Within the precincts of this sacred grove:
Yet in the distance, ever and anon,
I hear their horrid laughter, like the howl
Of famish'd wolves, beneath the tree wherein
The traveller hides. Without, encamp'd they lie,
And should I quit this consecrated grove,
Shaking their serpent locks, they would arise,
And, raising clouds of dust on every side,
Ceaseless pursue their miserable prey.

IPHIGENIA.

Orestes, canst thou hear a friendly word?

ORESTES.

Reserve it for one favour'd by the gods.

IPHIGENIA.

To thee they give anew the light of hope.

ORESTES.

Through clouds and smoke I see the feeble gleam
Of the death-stream which lights me down to hell.

IPHIGENIA.

Hast thou one sister only, thy Electra?

ORESTES.

I knew but one: yet her kind destiny,
Which seem'd to us so terrible, betimes
Removed an elder sister from the woe
That dogs the race of Pelops. Cease, oh cease
Thy questions, maiden, nor thus league thyself
With the Eumenides, who blow away,
With fiendish joy, the ashes from my soul,
Lest the last spark of horror's fiery brand
Should be extinguish'd there. Must then the fire,
Deliberately kindl'd and supplied
With hellish sulphur, never cease to sear
My tortur'd bosom?

IPHIGENIA.

In the flame I throw
Sweet incense. Let the gentle breath of love,
Low murmuring, cool thy bosom's fiery glow.
Orestes, fondly lov'd,—canst thou not hear me?
Hath the terrific Furies' grisly band
Completely dried the life-blood in thy veins?
Creeps there, as from the Gorgon's direful head,
A petrifying charm through all thy limbs?
If hollow voices, from a mother's blood,
Call thee to hell, may not a sister's word
With benediction pure ascend to heaven,
And summon thence some gracious power to aid thee?

ORESTES.

She calls! she calls!—Thou too desir'st my death?
Is there a fury shrouded in thy form?
Who art thou, that thy voice thus horribly
Can harrow up my bosom's inmost depths?

IPHIGENIA.

Thine inmost heart reveals it. I am she,
Iphigenia,—look on me, Orestes!

ORESTES.

Thou!

IPHIGENIA.

My own brother!

ORESTES.

Hence, away, begone!
Touch not these locks, I counsel thee; from me,
As from Creusa's bridal robe, proceeds
An unextinguishable fire. Depart!
Like Hercules, an ignominious death,
Unworthy wretch, look'd in myself, I'll die.

IPHIGENIA.

Thou shalt not perish! Would that I might hear
One quiet word from thee! dispel my doubts,
Make sure the bliss I have implor'd so long.
A wheel of joy and sorrow in my heart
Ceaseless revolves. With shy reserve I turn
From one unknown; but unto thee, my brother,
My inmost heart resistlessly impels me.

ORESTES.

Is this Lyæus' temple? Doth the glow
Of holy rage unbridl'd thus possess
The sacred priestess?

IPHIGENIA.

Hear me, oh, look up!
See how my heart, which hath been clos'd so long,
Doth open to the bliss of seeing thee,
The dearest treasure that the world contains,—
Of falling on thy neck, and folding thee
Within my longing arms, which have till now
Met the embraces of the empty wind.
Do not repulse me,—the eternal spring,
Whose crystal waters from Parnassus flow,
Bounds not more gaily on from rock to rock,
Down to the golden vale, than from my heart
The waters of affection freely gush,
And round me form a circling sea of bliss.
Orestes! Oh, my brother!

ORESTES.

Lovely nymph!
Nor thy caresses, nor thyself I trust;

Diana claims attendants more severe,
And doth avenge her desecrated fane.
Remove thy circling arm! and if thou wilt
Safety and love upon a youth bestow,
Unto my friend, more worthy than myself,
Impart thy gifts; among yon rocks he roves;
Go seek him, guide him hence, and heed not me.

IPHIGENIA.

Brother, command thyself, and better know
Thy new-found sister, nor misconstrue thus
Her pure and heav'nly joy. Ye Gods, remove
From his fix'd eye delusion, lest this hour
Of highest bliss should make us trebly wretched!
Oh she is here, thine own, thy long-lost sister,
Whom great Diana from the altar snatch'd,
And safely plac'd here in her sacred fane.
A captive thou, prepar'd for sacrifice,
And findest here a sister in the priestess.

ORESTES.

Accursed race! Now may the sun behold
Your final doom. Is not Electra here?
That she with us may perish, nor her life

For heavier doom and deeper woe reserve.
'Tis well,—I follow, priestess! Fratricide
Is an old custom of our ancient house;
And you, ye Gods, I thank, that ye resolve
Childless to root me hence. Thee let me counsel
To view too fondly neither sun nor stars.
Come follow to the gloomy realms below!
As dragons, gender'd in the sulphur pool,
Swallow each other with voracious rage,
So our accurs'd race destroys itself.
Childless and guiltless come below with me!
There's pity in thy look! oh, gaze not so,—
'Twas with such looks that Clytemnestra sought
An entrance to her son Orestes' heart,
And yet his uprais'd arm her bosom pierc'd.
His mother fell!—Appear, indignant shade!
Within the circle step, ye fiends of hell,
Be present at the welcome spectacle,
The last, most horrible, that ye prepare!

Nor hate, nor vengeance, whets the poignard now,
A sister is constrain'd to deal the blow.
Weep not! Thy guiltless soul is free from crime.
From earliest infancy I nought have lov'd,
As thee I could have lov'd, my sister. Come,
The weapon raise, spare not, this bosom rend,
And make an outlet for its boiling streams!

(He sinks exhausted.)

IPHIGENIA.

Alone I cannot bear this bliss and woe.
Where art thou, Pylades? Thine aid I need.

(Iphigenia retires.)

SCENE II.

ORESTES.

Recovering from his swoon and standing up.

Give yet another! reach from Lethe's stream

43

The last reviving draught of cool refreshment!
Soon shall its waters in my bosom still
Life's fitful fever; and my spirit then
Adown oblivion's stream shall glide to you,
Ye spirits, shrouded in eternal mist.
With tranquil pleasure in your deep repose
A weary son of earth may lave his soul!—
What whisp'ring sounds pervade the dreary grove?
What hollow murmurs haunt its twilight gloom?—
They gather round to view the stranger guest!
Who are yon troop in high communion met,
Like an assembl'd family of princes?
They mingle peacefully, of every age,
And either sex, yet are their godlike forms
Cast in a kindred mould. 'Tis they, 'tis they,
The fathers of my race! With Atreus,
In friendly converse glides Thyestes' shade,
And children playfully around them sport.
Is there no enmity among you now?
And is revenge extinguish'd with the sun?
I then am welcome, and may hope to join
Your solemn company. My fathers, hail!
Orestes, last descendant of your race,
Salutes you. What ye sow'd, that hath he reap'd

Laden with curses he descends to you.
But burdens here are lighter far to bear.
Receive him, oh, receive him in your circle!
Thee, Atreus, I revere, and thee, Thyestes:
Here all are free from enmity and hate.—
Show me my father, whom I only once
In life beheld.—Art thou my father, thou,
My mother leading thus familiarly?
Dares Clytemnestra reach her hand to thee;
Then may Orestes also draw near her,
And say, behold thy son!—My ancestors,
Behold your son, and bid him welcome here,
Among the sons of ancient Tantalus,
A kind salute on earth was murder's watchword,
And all their joys commence beyond the grave.
Ye welcome me! Ye bid me join your circle!
Oh, lead me to my honour'd ancestor!

Where is the aged hero? that I may
Behold the dear, the venerable head,
Of him, who with the gods in council sat.
You seem to shudder and to turn away?
What may this mean? Suffers the godlike man?
Alas! the mighty gods, with ruthless hate,
To his heroic breast, with brazen chains,
Have cruel pangs indissolubly bound.

SCENE III.

ORESTES.   IPHIGENIA.   PYLADES.

ORESTES.

How! are ye come already? Sister, welcome.
Electra still is missing: some kind god
With gentle arrow send her quickly hither.
Thee, my poor friend, I must compassionate!
Come with me, come to Pluto's gloomy throne.
There to salute our hosts like stranger guests.

IPHIGENIA.

Celestial pair, who from the realms above
By night and day shed down the beauteous light
To cheer mankind, but who may not illume
Departed spirits, save a mortal pair!

A brother's and a sister's anguish pity!
For thou, Diana, lov'st thy gentle brother
Beyond what earth and heaven can offer thee
And dost, with quiet yearning, ever turn
Thy virgin face to his eternal light.
Let not my only brother, found so late,
Rave in the darkness of insanity!
And is thy will, when thou didst here conceal me,
At length fulfill'd,—would'st thou to me through him,
To him through me, thy gracious aid extend,—
Oh, free him from the fetters of this curse,
Lest vainly pass the precious hours of safety.

PYLADES.

Dost thou not know us, and this sacred grove,
And this blest light, which shines not on the dead?
Dost thou not feel thy sister and thy friend,
Who hold thee living in their firm embrace?
Grasp us! we are not shadows. Mark my words!
Collect thyself,—each moment now is precious,
And our return hangs on a slender thread,
Which, as it seems, some gracious fate doth spin.

ORESTES *to* IPHIGENIA.

My sister, let me for the first time taste,
With open heart, pure joy within thine arms!
Ye gods, who charge the heavy clouds with dread,
And sternly gracious send the long-sought rain
With thunder and the rush of mighty winds,
A horrid deluge on the trembling earth;
Yet dissipate at length man's dread suspense,
Exchanging timid wonder's anxious gaze
For grateful looks and joyous songs of praise,
When in each sparkling drop which gems the leaves,
Apollo, thousand-fold, reflects his beam,
And Iris colours with a magic hand
The dusky texture of the parting clouds;
Oh, let me also in my sister's arms,
And on the bosom of my friend, enjoy
With grateful thanks the bliss ye now bestow
My heart assures me that your curses cease.
The dread Eumenides at length retire,
The brazen gates of Tartarus I hear

Behind them closing with a thund'ring clang.
A quick'ning odour from the earth ascends,
Inviting me to chase, upon its plains,
The joys of life and deeds of high emprise.

PYLADES.

Lose not the moments which are limited!
The favouring gale, which swells our parting sail,
Must to Olympus waft our perfect joy.
Quick counsel and resolve the time demands.

ACT THE FOURTH.

SCENE I.

IPHIGENIA.

When the Powers on high decree
For a feeble child of earth
Dire perplexity and woe,
And his spirit doom to pass
With tumult wild from joy to grief,
And back again from grief to joy,
In fearful alternation;
They in mercy then provide,
In the precincts of his home,
Or upon the distant shore,
That to him may never fail
Ready help in hours of need,
A tranquil, faithful friend.
Oh, bless, ye heavenly powers, our Pylades,
And every project that his mind may form!
In combat his the vigorous arm of youth,
And in the counsel his the eye of age.
His soul is tranquil; in his inner mind
He guards a sacred, undisturb'd repose,
And from its silent depths a rich supply
Of aid and counsel draws for the distress'd.
He tore me from my brother, upon whom,
With fond amaze, I gaz'd and gaz'd again;
I could not realize my happiness,
Nor loose him from my arms, and heeded not
The danger's near approach that threatens us.
To execute their project of escape,

They hasten to the sea, where in a bay
Their comrades in the vessel lie conceal'd
And wait a signal. Me they have supplied
With artful answers, should the monarch send
To urge the sacrifice. Alas! I see
I must consent to follow like a child.

I have not learn'd deception, nor the art
To gain with crafty wiles my purposes.
Detested falsehood! it doth not relieve
The breast like words of truth: it comforts not,
But is a torment in the forger's heart,
And, like an arrow which a god directs,
Flies back and wounds the archer. Through my heart
One fear doth chase another; perhaps with rage,
Again on the unconsecrated shore,
The Furies' grisly band my brother seize.
Perchance they are surpris'd? Methinks I hear
The tread of armed men. A messenger
Is coming from the king, with hasty steps.
How throbs my heart, how troubl'd is my soul
Now that I see the countenance of one,
Whom with a word untrue I must encounter!

SCENE II.

IPHIGENIA.   ARKAS.

ARKAS.

Priestess, with speed conclude the sacrifice,
Impatiently the king and people wait.

IPHIGENIA.

I had perform'd my duty and thy will,
Had not an unforeseen impediment
The execution of my purpose thwarted.

ARKAS.

What is it that obstructs the king's commands?

IPHIGENIA.

Chance, which from mortals will not brook control.

ARKAS.

Possess me with the reason, that with speed
I may inform the king, who hath decreed
The death of both.

48

IPHIGENIA.

The gods have not decreed it.
The elder of these men doth bear the guilt
Of kindred murder; on his steps attend
The dread Eumenides. They seiz'd their prey
Within the inner fane, polluting thus
The holy sanctuary. I hasten now,
Together with my virgin-train, to bathe
Diana's image in the sea, and there
With solemn rites its purity restore.
Let none presume our silent march to follow!

ARKAS.

This hindrance to the monarch I'll announce:
Do not commence the rite till he permit.

IPHIGENIA.

The priestess interferes alone in this.

ARKAS.

An incident so strange the king should know.

IPHIGENIA.

Here, nor his counsel nor command avails.

ARKAS.

Oft are the great consulted out of form.

IPHIGENIA.

Do not insist on what I must refuse.

ARKAS.

A needful and a just demand refuse not.

IPHIGENIA.

I yield, if thou delay not.

ARKAS.

I with speed
Will bear these tidings to the camp, and soon
Acquaint thee, priestess, with the king's reply.
There is a message I would gladly bear him:

'Twould quickly banish all perplexity:
Thou didst not heed thy faithful friend's advice.

IPHIGENIA.

I willingly have done whate'er I could.

ARKAS.

E'en now 'tis not too late to change thy mind.

IPHIGENIA.

To do so is, alas, beyond our power.

ARKAS.

What thou wouldst shun, thou deem'st impossible.

IPHIGENIA.

Thy wish doth make thee deem it possible.

ARKAS.

Wilt thou so calmly venture everything?

IPHIGENIA.

My fate I have committed to the gods.

ARKAS.

The gods are wont to save by human means.

IPHIGENIA.

By their appointment everything is done.

ARKAS.

Believe me, all doth now depend on thee.
The irritated temper of the king
Alone condemns these men to bitter death.
The soldiers from the cruel sacrifice
And bloody service long have been disused;
Nay, many, whom their adverse fortunes cast
In foreign regions, there themselves have felt
How godlike to the exil'd wanderer
The friendly countenance of man appears.
Do not deprive us of thy gentle aid!
With ease thou canst thy sacred task fulfil:
For nowhere doth benignity, which comes

In human form from heaven, so quickly gain
An empire o'er the heart, as where a race,
Gloomy and savage, full of life and power,
Without external guidance, and oppress'd
With vague forebodings, bear life's heavy load.

IPHIGENIA.

Shake not my spirit, which thou canst not bend
According to thy will.

ARKAS.

                    While there is time
Nor labour nor persuasion shall be spar'd.

IPHIGENIA.

Thy labour but occasions pain to me;
Both are in vain; therefore, I pray, depart.

ARKAS.

I summon pain to aid me, 'tis a friend
Who counsels wisely.

IPHIGENIA.

                    Though it shakes my soul,
It doth not banish thence my strong repugnance.

ARKAS.

Can then a gentle soul repugnance feel
For benefits bestow'd by one so noble?

IPHIGENIA.

Yes, when the donor, for those benefits,
Instead of gratitude, demands myself.

ARKAS.

Who no affection feels doth never want
Excuses. To the king I'll now relate
All that has happen'd. Oh, that in thy soul
Thou wouldst revolve his noble conduct, priestess,
Since thy arrival to the present day!

SCENE III.

IPHIGENIA, *alone.*

These words at an unseasonable hour
Produce a strong revulsion in my breast;
I am alarm'd!—For as the rushing tide
In rapid currents eddies o'er the rocks
Which lie among the sand upon the shore;
E'en so a stream of joy o'erwhelm'd my soul.
I grasp'd what had appear'd impossible.
It was as though another gentle cloud
Around me lay, to raise me from the earth,
And rock my spirit in the same sweet sleep
Which the kind goddess shed around my brow,
What time her circling arm from danger snatch'd me.
My brother forcibly engross'd my heart;
I listen'd only to his friend's advice;
My soul rush'd eagerly to rescue them,
And as the mariner with joy surveys
The less'ning breakers of a desert isle,
So Tauris lay behind me. But the voice
Of faithful Arkas wakes me from my dream,

Reminding me that those whom I forsake
Are also men. Deceit doth now become
Doubly detested. O my soul, be still!
Beginn'st thou now to tremble and to doubt?
Thy lonely shelter on the firm-set earth
Must thou abandon? and, embark'd once more,
At random drift upon tumultuous waves,
A stranger to thyself and to the world?

SCENE IV.

IPHIGENIA.   PYLADES.

PYLADES.

Where is she? that my words with speed may tell
The joyful tidings of our near escape!

IPHIGENIA.

Oppress'd with gloomy care, I much require
The certain comfort thou dost promise me.

PYLADES.

Thy brother is restor'd! The rocky paths
Of this unconsecrated shore we trod
In friendly converse, while behind us lay,
Unmark'd by us, the consecrated grove;
And ever with increasing glory shone
The fire of youth around his noble brow.
Courage and hope his glowing eye inspir'd;
And his free heart exulted with the joy
Of saving thee, his sister, and his friend.

IPHIGENIA.

The gods shower blessings on thee, Pylades!
And from those lips which breathe such welcome news,
Be the sad note of anguish never heard!

PYLADES.

I bring yet more,—for Fortune, like a prince,
Comes not alone, but well accompanied.
Our friends and comrades we have also found.
Within a bay they had conceal'd the ship,
And mournful sat expectant. They beheld
Thy brother, and a joyous shout uprais'd,
Imploring him to haste the parting hour.
Each hand impatient long'd to grasp the oar,

While from the shore a gently murmuring breeze,
Perceiv'd by all, unfurl'd its wing auspicious.
Let us then hasten; guide me to the fane,
That I may tread the sanctuary, and seize
With sacred awe the object of our hopes.
I can unaided on my shoulder bear
Diana's image: how I long to feel
The precious burden!

> [*While speaking the last words, he approaches
> the Temple, without perceiving that he is*
>
not
>
> *followed by Iphigenia: at length he turns*

round.]

Why thus ling'ring stand.
Why art thou silent? wherefore thus confus'd?
Doth some new obstacle oppose our bliss?
Inform me, hast thou to the king announc'd
The prudent message we agreed upon?

IPHIGENIA.

I have, dear Pylades; yet wilt thou chide.
Thy very aspect is a mute reproach.
The royal messenger arriv'd, and I,
According to thy counsel, fram'd my speech.
He seem'd surpris'd, and urgently besought,
That to the monarch I should first announce
The rite unusual, and attend his will.
I now await the messenger's return.

PYLADES.

Danger again doth hover o'er our heads!
O priestess, why neglect to shroud thyself
Within the veil of sacerdotal rites?

IPHIGENIA.

I never have employ'd them as a veil.

PYLADES.

Pure soul! thy scruples will destroy alike
Thyself and us. Why did I not foresee
Such an emergency, and tutor thee
This counsel also wisely to elude?

IPHIGENIA.

Chide only me, for mine alone the blame.
Yet other answer could I not return
To him, who strongly and with reason urg'd
What my own heart acknowledg'd to be right.

PYLADES.

The danger thickens; but let us be firm,
Nor with incautious haste betray ourselves;
Calmly await the messenger's return,

And then stand fast, whatever his reply:
For the appointment of such sacred rites
Doth to the priestess, not the king belong.
Should he demand the stranger to behold
Who is by madness heavily oppress'd,
Evasively pretend, that in the fane,
Securely guarded, thou retain'st us both.
Thus you secure us time to fly with speed,
Bearing the sacred treasure from this race,
Unworthy its possession. Phœbus sends
Auspicious omens, and fulfils his word,
Ere we the first conditions have perform'd.
Free is Orestes, from the curse absolv'd!
Oh, with the freed one, to the rocky isle
Where dwells the god, waft us, propitious gales!
Thence to Mycene, that she may revive;
That from the ashes of the extinguish'd hearth,
The household gods may joyously arise,
And beauteous fire illumine their abode!
Thy hand from golden censers first shall strew
The fragrant incense. O'er that threshold thou
Shalt life and blessing once again dispense,
The curse atone, and all thy kindred grace
With the fresh bloom of renovated life.

IPHIGENIA.

As doth the flower revolve to meet the sun,
Once more my spirit to sweet comfort turns,
Struck by thy words' invigorating ray.
How dear the counsel of a present friend,
Lacking whose godlike power, the lonely one
In silence droops! for, lock'd within his breast,
Slowly are ripen'd purpose and resolve,
Which friendship's genial warmth had soon matur'd.

PYLADES.

Farewell! I haste to re-assure our friends,
Who anxiously await us: then with speed
I will return, and, hid within the brake,

Attend thy signal.—Wherefore, all at once,
Doth anxious thought o'ercloud thy brow serene?

IPHIGENIA.

Forgive me! As light clouds athwart the sun,
So cares and fears float darkling o'er my soul.

PYLADES.

Oh, banish fear! With danger it hath form'd
A close alliance,—they are constant friends.

IPHIGENIA.

It is an honest scruple, which forbids
That I should cunningly deceive the king,
And plunder him who was my second sire.

PYLADES.

Him thou dost fly, who would have slain thy brother.

IPHIGENIA.

To me, at least, he hath been ever kind.

PYLADES.

What Fate commands is not ingratitude.

IPHIGENIA.

Alas! it still remains ingratitude;
Necessity alone can justify it.

PYLADES.

Thee, before gods and men it justifies.

IPHIGENIA.

But my own heart is still unsatisfied.

PYLADES.

Scruples too rigid are a cloak for pride.

IPHIGENIA.

I cannot argue, I can only feel.

PYLADES.

Conscious of right, thou shouldst respect thyself.

IPHIGENIA.

Then only doth the heart know perfect ease,

When not a stain pollutes it.

PYLADES.

In this fane
Pure hast thou kept thy heart. Life teaches us
To be less strict with others and ourselves;
Thou'lt learn the lesson too. So wonderful
Is human nature, and its varied ties
Are so involv'd and complicate, that none

May hope to keep his inmost spirit pure,
And walk without perplexity through life.
Nor are we call'd upon to judge ourselves;
With circumspection to pursue his path,
Is the immediate duty of a man.
For seldom can he rightly estimate,
Or his past conduct or his present deeds.

IPHIGENIA.

Almost thou dost persuade me to consent.

PYLADES.

Needs there persuasion when no choice is granted?
To save thyself, thy brother, and a friend,
One path presents itself, and canst thou ask
If we shall follow it?

IPHIGENIA.

Still let me pause,
For such injustice thou couldst not thyself
Calmly return for benefits receiv'd.

PYLADES.

If we should perish, bitter self-reproach,
Forerunner of despair, will be thy portion.
It seems thou art not used to suffer much,
When, to escape so great calamity,
Thou canst refuse to utter one false word.

IPHIGENIA.

Oh, that I bore within a manly heart!
Which, when it hath conceiv'd a bold resolve,
'Gainst every other voice doth close itself.

PYLADES.

In vain thou dost refuse; with iron hand
Necessity commands; her stern decree
Is law supreme, to which the gods themselves
Must yield submission. In dread silence rules
The uncounsell'd sister of eternal fate.
What she appoints thee to endure,—endure;
What to perform,—perform. The rest thou know'st.
Ere long I will return, and then receive
The seal of safety from thy sacred hand.

SCENE V.

IPHIGENIA, *alone*.

I must obey him, for I see my friends
Beset with peril. Yet my own sad fate
Doth with increasing anguish move my heart.
May I no longer feed the silent hope
Which in my solitude I fondly cherish'd?
Shall the dire curse eternally endure?
And shall our fated race ne'er rise again
With blessings crown'd?—All mortal things decay!
The noblest powers, the purest joys of life
At length subside: then wherefore not the curse?
And have I vainly hop'd that, guarded here,
Secluded from the fortunes of my race,
I, with pure heart and hands, some future day
Might cleanse the deep defilement of our house?
Scarce was my brother in my circling arms
From raging madness suddenly restor'd,
Scarce had the ship, long pray'd for, near'd the strand,
Once more to waft me to my native shores,
When unrelenting fate, with iron hand,
A double crime enjoins; commanding me
To steal the image, sacred and rever'd,
Confided to my care, and him deceive
To whom I owe my life and destiny.
Let not abhorrence spring within my heart!
Nor the old Titan's hate, toward you, ye gods,

Infix its vulture talons in my breast!
Save me, and save your image in my soul!
An ancient song comes back upon mine ear—
I had forgotten it, and willingly—
The Parcæ's song, which horribly they sang,
What time, hurl'd headlong from his golden seat,
Fell Tantalus. They with their noble friend
Keen anguish suffer'd; savage was their breast
And horrible their song. In days gone by,
When we were children, oft our ancient nurse
Would sing it to us, and I mark'd it well.

            Oh, fear the immortals,
            Ye children of men!
            Eternal dominion
            They hold in their hands.
            And o'er their wide empire
            Wield absolute sway.
            Whom they have exalted
            Let him fear them most!
            Around golden tables,
            On cliffs and clouds resting
            The seats are prepar'd.
            If contest ariseth;
            The guests are hurl'd headlong,
            Disgrac'd and dishonour'd,
            And fetter'd in darkness,
            Await with vain longing,
            A juster decree.
            But in feasts everlasting,
            Around the gold tables
            Still dwell the immortals.
            From mountain to mountain
            They stride; while ascending
            From fathomless chasms,
            The breath of the Titans,
            Half stifl'd with anguish,
            Like volumes of incense
            Fumes up to the skies.
            From races ill-fated,
            Their aspect joy-bringing,
            Oft turn the celestials,

And shun in the children
To gaze on the features
Once lov'd and still speaking
Of their mighty sire.
Thus sternly the Fates sang
Immur'd in his dungeon.
The banish'd one listens,
The song of the Parcæ,
His children's doom ponders,
And boweth his head.

ACT THE FIFTH.

SCENE I.

THOAS.　　ARKAS.

ARKAS.

I own I am perplex'd, and scarcely know
'Gainst whom to point the shaft of my suspicion,
Whether the priestess aids the captives' flight,
Or they themselves clandestinely contrive it.
'Tis rumour'd that the ship which brought them here
Is lurking somewhere in a bay conceal'd.
This stranger's madness, these new lustral rites,
The specious pretext for delay, excite
Mistrust, and call aloud for vigilance.

THOAS.

Summon the priestess to attend me here!
Then go with speed, and strictly search the shore,
From yon projecting land to Dian's grove:
Forbear to violate its sacred depths;
A watchful ambush set, attack and seize,
According to your wont, whome'er ye find.

[Arkas retires.

SCENE II.

THOAS, *alone*.

Fierce anger rages in my riven breast,
First against her, whom I esteem'd so pure;
Then 'gainst myself, whose foolish lenity
Hath fashion'd her for treason. Man is soon
Inur'd to slavery, and quickly learns
Submission, when of freedom quite depriv'd.

If she had fallen in the savage hands
Of my rude sires, and had their holy rage
Forborne to slay her, grateful for her life,
She would have recogniz'd her destiny.
Have shed before the shrine the stranger's blood,
And duty nam'd what was necessity.
Now my forbearance in her breast allures
Audacious wishes. Vainly I had hop'd

To bind her to me; rather she contrives
To shape an independent destiny.
She won my heart through flattery; and now
That I oppose her, seeks to gain her ends
By fraud and cunning, and my kindness deems
A worthless and prescriptive property.

SCENE III.

IPHIGENIA.   THOAS.

IPHIGENIA.

Me hast thou summon'd? wherefore art thou here?

THOAS.

Wherefore delay the sacrifice? inform me.

IPHIGENIA.

I have acquainted Arkas with the reasons.

THOAS.

From thee I wish to hear them more at large.

IPHIGENIA.

The goddess for reflection grants thee time.

THOAS.

To thee this time seems also opportune.

IPHIGENIA.

If to this cruel deed thy heart is steel'd,
Thou shouldst not come! A king who meditates
A deed inhuman, may find slaves enow,
Willing for hire to bear one half the curse,
And leave the monarch's presence undefil'd.
Enwrapt in gloomy clouds he forges death,
Whose flaming arrow on his victim's head
His hirelings hurl; while he above the storm
Remains untroubl'd, an impassive god.

THOAS.

A wild song, priestess, issued from thy lips.

IPHIGENIA.

No priestess, king! but Agamemnon's daughter;
While yet unknown, thou didst respect my words:
A princess now,—and think'st thou to command me
From youth I have been tutor'd to obey,
My parents first, and then the deity;

And thus obeying, ever hath my soul
Known sweetest freedom. But nor then nor now
Have I been taught compliance with the voice
And savage mandates of a man.

THOAS.

Not I,
An ancient law doth claim obedience from thee.

IPHIGENIA.

Our passions eagerly catch hold of laws
Which they can wield as weapons. But to me
Another law, one far more ancient, speaks,
And doth command me to withstand thee, king!
That law declaring sacred every stranger.

THOAS.

These men, methinks, lie very near thy heart.
When sympathy with them can lead thee thus
To violate discretion's primal law,
That those in power should never be provok'd.

IPHIGENIA.

Speaking or silent, thou canst always know
What is, and ever must be, in my heart.
Doth not remembrance of a common doom,
To soft compassion melt the hardest heart?
How much more mine! in them I see myself.
I trembling kneel'd before the altar once.
And solemnly the shade of early death
Environ'd me. Aloft the knife was rais'd
To pierce my bosom, throbbing with warm life;
A dizzy horror overwhelm'd my soul;
My eyes grew dim;—I found myself in safety.
Are we not bound to render the distress'd
The gracious kindness from the gods receiv'd?
Thou know'st we are, and yet wilt thou compel me?

THOAS.

Obey thine office, priestess, not the king.

IPHIGENIA.

Cease! nor thus seek to cloak the savage force
Which triumphs o'er a woman's feebleness.
Though woman, I am born as free as man.
Did Agamemnon's son before thee stand,
And thou requiredst what became him not,

His arm and trusty weapon would defend

His bosom's freedom. I have only words
But it becomes a noble-minded man
To treat with due respect the words of woman.

THOAS.

I more respect them than a brother's sword.

IPHIGENIA.

Uncertain ever is the chance of arms,
No prudent warrior doth despise his foe;
Nor yet defenceless 'gainst severity
Hath nature left the weak; she gives him craft
And wily cunning: artful he delays,
Evades, eludes, and finally escapes.
Such arms are justified by violence.

THOAS.

But circumspection countervails deceit.

IPHIGENIA.

Which a pure spirit doth abhor to use.

THOAS.

Do not incautiously condemn thyself.

IPHIGENIA.

Oh, couldst thou see the struggle of my soul,
Courageously to ward the first attack
Of an unhappy doom, which threatens me!
Do I then stand before thee weaponless?
Prayer, lovely prayer, fair branch in woman's hand,
More potent far than instruments of war,
Thou dost thrust back. What now remains for me
Wherewith my inborn freedom to defend?
Must I implore a miracle from heaven?
Is there no power within my spirit's depths?

THOAS.

Extravagant thy interest in the fate
Of these two strangers. Tell me who they are,
For whom thy heart is thus so deeply mov'd.

IPHIGENIA.

They are—they seem at least—I think them Greeks.

THOAS.

Thy countrymen; no doubt they have renew'd
The pleasing picture of return.

IPHIGENIA, *after a pause.*

                    Doth man
Lay undisputed claim to noble deeds?
Doth he alone to his heroic breast
Clasp the impossible? What call we great?
What deeds, though oft narrated, still uplift
With shudd'ring horror the narrator's soul,
But those which, with improbable success,
The valiant have attempted? Shall the man
Who all alone steals on his foes by night,
And raging like an unexpected fire,
Destroys the slumbering host, and press'd at length
By rous'd opponents or his foemen's steeds,
Retreats with booty—be alone extoll'd?
Or he who, scorning safety, boldly roams
Through woods and dreary wilds, to scour the land
Of thieves and robbers? Is nought left for us?
Must gentle woman quite forego her nature,—
Force against force employ,—like Amazons,
Usurp the sword from man, and bloodily
Revenge oppression? In my heart I feel
The stirrings of a noble enterprize;
But if I fail—severe reproach, alas!
And bitter misery will be my doom.
Thus on my knees I supplicate the gods.
Oh, are ye truthful, as men say ye are,
Now prove it by your countenance and aid;
Honour the truth in me! Attend, O king!
A secret plot is laid; 'tis vain to ask
Touching the captives; they are gone, and seek
Their comrades who await them on the shore.
The eldest,—he whom madness lately seiz'd,
And who is now recover'd,—is Orestes,
My brother, and the other Pylades,
His early friend and faithful confidant.
From Delphi, Phœbus sent them to this shore

With a divine command to steal away
The image of Diana, and to him
Bear back the sister, promising for this
Redemption to the blood-stain'd matricide.
I have deliver'd now into thy hands

The remnants of the house of Tantalus.
Destroy us—if thou canst.

THOAS.

And dost thou think
The savage Scythian will attend the voice
Of truth and of humanity, unheard
By the Greek Atreus?

IPHIGENIA.

'Tis heard by all,
Whate'er may be their clime, within whose breast
Flows pure and free the gushing stream of life.—
What silent purpose broods within thy soul?
Is it destruction? Let me perish first!
For now, deliv'rance hopeless, I perceive
The dreadful peril into which I have
With rash precipitancy plung'd my friends.
Alas! I soon shall see them bound before me!
How to my brother shall I say farewell?
I, the unhappy author of his death.
Ne'er can I gaze again in his dear eyes!

THOAS.

The traitors have contriv'd a cunning web,
And cast it round thee, who, secluded long,
Giv'st willing credence to thine own desires.

IPHIGENIA.

No, no! I'd pledge my life these men are true.
And shouldst thou find them otherwise, O king,
Then let them perish both, and cast me forth,
That on some rock-girt island's dreary shore
I may atone my folly. Are they true,
And is this man indeed my dear Orestes,
My brother, long implor'd,—release us both,
And o'er us stretch the kind protecting arm,

Which long hath shelter'd me. My noble sire
Fell through his consort's guilt,—she by her son;
On him alone the hope of Atreus' race
Doth now repose. Oh, with pure heart and hands
Let me depart to expiate our house.
Yes, thou wilt keep thy promise; thou didst swear,
That were a safe return provided me,
I should be free to go. The hour is come.

A king doth never grant like common men,
Merely to gain a respite from petition;
Nor promise what he hopes will ne'er be claim'd.
Then first he feels his dignity complete
When he can make the long-expecting happy.

THOAS.

As fire opposes water, and doth seek
With hissing rage to overcome its foe,
So doth my anger strive against thy words.

IPHIGENIA.

Let mercy, like the consecrated flame
Of silent sacrifice, encircl'd round
With songs of gratitude, and joy, and praise,
Above the tumult gently rise to heaven.

THOAS.

How often hath this voice assuag'd my soul!

IPHIGENIA.

Extend thy hand to me in sign of peace.

THOAS.

Large thy demand within so short a time.

IPHIGENIA.

Beneficence doth no reflection need.

THOAS.

'Tis needed oft, for evil springs from good.

IPHIGENIA.

'Tis doubt which good doth oft to evil turn.

Consider not: act as thy feelings prompt thee.

SCENE IV.

ORESTES (*armed*).   IPHIGENIA.   THOAS.

ORESTES, *addressing his followers.*

Redouble your exertions! hold them back!
Few moments will suffice; retain your ground,
And keep a passage open to the ship
For me and for my sister.

To **IPHIGENIA,** *without perceiving* **THOAS.**

Come with speed!
We are betray'd,—brief time remains for flight.

THOAS.

None in my presence with impunity
His naked weapon wears.

IPHIGENIA.

Do not profane
Diana's sanctuary with rage and blood.
Command your people to forbear awhile,
And listen to the priestess, to the sister.

ORESTES.

Say, who is he that threatens us?

IPHIGENIA.

In him
Revere the king, who was my second father.
Forgive me, brother, that my childlike heart
Hath plac'd our fate thus wholly in his hands.
I have betray'd your meditated flight,
And thus from treachery redeem'd my soul.

ORESTES.

Will he permit our peaceable return?

IPHIGENIA.

Thy gleaming sword forbids me to reply.

ORESTES, *sheathing his sword.*

Then speak! thou seest I listen to thy words.

SCENE V.

ORESTES. IPHIGENIA. THOAS.

Enter PYLADES, *soon after him* ARKAS, *both with drawn swords.*

PYLADES.

Do not delay! our friends are putting forth
Their final strength, and yielding step by step,
Are slowly driven backward to the sea.—
A conference of princes find I here?
Is this the sacred person of the king?

ARKAS.

Calmly, as doth become thee, thou dost stand,
O king, surrounded by thine enemies.
Soon their temerity shall be chastis'd;
Their yielding followers fly.—their ship is ours.
Speak but the word, and it is wrapt in flames.

THOAS.

Go, and command my people to forbear!
Let none annoy the foe while we confer.   (*Arkas retires.*)

ORESTES.

I willingly consent. Go, Pylades!
Collect the remnant of our friends, and wait
The appointed issue of our enterprize.

(*Pylades retires.*)

SCENE VI.

IPHIGENIA. THOAS. ORESTES.

IPHIGENIA.

Believe my cares ere ye begin to speak.
I fear contention, if thou wilt not hear
The voice of equity, O king,—if thou
Wilt not, my brother, curb thy headstrong youth.

THOAS.

I, as becomes the elder, check my rage.
Now answer me: how dost thou prove thyself
The priestess' brother, Agamemnon's son?

ORESTES.

Behold the sword with which the hero slew
The valiant Trojans. From his murderer
I took the weapon, and implor'd the Gods
To grant me Agamemnon's mighty arm,
Success, and valour, with a death more noble.
Select one of the leaders of thy host,
And place the best as my opponent here.
Where'er on earth the sons of heroes dwell,
This boon is to the stranger ne'er refus'd.

THOAS.

This privilege hath ancient custom here
To strangers ne'er accorded.

ORESTES.

Then from us
Commence the novel custom! A whole race
In imitation soon will consecrate
Its monarch's noble action into law.
Nor let me only for our liberty,—
Let me, a stranger, for all strangers fight.

If I should fall, my doom be also theirs;
But if kind fortune crown me with success,
Let none e'er tread this shore, and fail to meet
The beaming eye of sympathy and love,
Or unconsol'd depart!

THOAS.

Thou dost not seem
Unworthy of thy boasted ancestry.

Great is the number of the valiant men
Who wait upon me; but I will myself,
Although advanc'd in years, oppose the foe,
And am prepar'd to try the chance of arms.

IPHIGENIA.

No, no! such bloody proofs are not requir'd.
Unhand thy weapon, king! my lot consider;
Rash combat oft immortalizes man;
If he should fall, he is renown'd in song;
But after ages reckon not the tears
Which ceaseless the forsaken woman sheds;
And poets tell not of the thousand nights
Consum'd in weeping, and the dreary days,
Wherein her anguish't soul, a prey to grief,
Doth vainly yearn to call her lov'd one back.
Fear warn'd me to beware lest robber's wiles
Might lure me from this sanctuary, and then
Betray me into bondage. Anxiously
I question'd them, each circumstance explor'd,
Demanded signs, and now my heart's assur'd.
See here, the mark as of three stars impress'd
On his right hand, which on his natal day
Were by the priest declar'd to indicate
Some dreadful deed by him to be perform'd.
And then this scar, which doth his eyebrow cleave,
Redoubles my conviction. When a child,
Electra, rash and inconsiderate,
Such was her nature, loos'd him from her arms.
He fell against a tripos. Oh, 'tis he!—
Shall I adduce the likeness to his sire,
Or the deep rapture of my inmost heart,
In further token of assurance, king?

THOAS.

E'en though thy words had banish'd every doubt,
And I had curb'd the anger in my breast,
Still must our arms decide. I see no peace.
Their purpose, as thou didst thyself confess,
Was to deprive me of Diana's image.
And think ye that I'll look contented on?
The Greeks are wont to cast a longing eye

Upon the treasures of barbarians,
A golden fleece, good steeds, or daughters fair;
But force and guile not always have avail'd
To lead them, with their booty, safely home.

ORESTES.

The image shall not be a cause of strife!
We now perceive the error which the God,
Our journey here commanding, like a veil,
Threw o'er our minds. His counsel I implor'd,
To free me from the Furies' grisly band.
He answer'd, "Back to Greece the sister bring,
Who in the sanctuary on Tauris' shore
Unwillingly abides; so ends the curse!"
To Phœbus' sister we applied the words,
And he referr'd to thee! The bonds severe,
Which held thee from us, holy one, are rent,
And thou art ours once more. At thy blest touch,
I felt myself restor'd. Within thine arms,
Madness once more around me coil'd its folds,
Crushing the marrow in my frame, and then
For ever, like a serpent, fled to hell.
Through thee, the daylight gladdens me anew.
The counsel of the Goddess now shines forth
In all its beauty and beneficence.
Like to a sacred image, unto which
An oracle immutably hath bound
A city's welfare, thee Diana took,
Protectress of our house, and guarded here
Within this holy stillness, to become
A blessing to thy brother and thy race.
Now when each passage to escape seems clos'd,
And safety hopeless, thou dost give us all.

O king, incline thine heart to thoughts of peace!
Let her fulfil her mission, and complete
The consecration of our father's house.
Me to their purified abode restore,
And place upon my brow the ancient crown!
Requite the blessing which her presence brought thee,
And let me now my nearer right enjoy!
Cunning and force, the proudest boast of man,

Fade in the lustre of her perfect truth;
Nor unrequited will a noble mind
Leave confidence, so childlike and so pure.

IPHIGENIA.

Think on thy promise; let thy heart be mov'd
By what a true and honest tongue hath spoken!
Look on us, king! an opportunity
For such a noble deed not oft occurs.
Refuse thou canst not,—give thy quick consent.

THOAS.

Then go!

IPHIGENIA.

    Not so, my king! I cannot part
Without thy blessing, or in anger from thee.
Banish us not! the sacred right of guests
Still let us claim: so not eternally
Shall we be sever'd. Honour'd and belov'd
As mine own father was, art thou by me:
And this impression in my soul remains.
Should e'en the meanest peasant of thy land
Bring to my ear the tones I heard from thee
Or should I on the humblest see thy garb,
I will with joy receive him as a god,
Prepare his couch myself, beside our hearth
Invite him to a seat, and only ask
Touching thy fate and thee. Oh, may the gods
To thee the merited reward impart
Of all thy kindness and benignity!
Farewell! Oh, do not turn away, but give
One kindly word of parting in return!
So shall the wind more gently swell our sails,

And from our eyes with soften'd anguish flow
The tears of separation. Fare thee well!
And graciously extend to me thy hand,
In pledge of ancient friendship.

THOAS, *extending his hand.*

    Fare thee well!

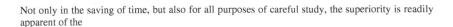

Not only in the saving of time, but also for all purposes of careful study, the superiority is readily apparent of the

Interlinear Translations

over other translations. For the self-teaching student and also for the hard-pressed teacher they make possible as well as convenient and easy, a correct solution of idioms, a quick insight into the sense, a facile and lucid re-arrangement of the context in the English order, and a practical comparison of both the similarities and the contrasts of construction. See other pages for the several titles and the prices, also for list of

Literal Translations,

Dictionaries, and other Specialties for teachers and students.

HANDY LITERAL TRANSLATIONS.

"To one who is reading the Classics, a literal translation is a convenient and legitimate help; and every well-informed person will read the Classics either in the original or in a translation."

Fifty-five volumes are now ready in this popular series, uniform in style and price. *For advertisement of new series of Interlinear Translations see end of this volume.*

Cæsar's Gallic War. *The 7 Books.*

Cicero's Defence of Roscius.

Cicero On Old Age and Friendship.

Cicero On Oratory.

Cicero On the Nature of the Gods.

Cicero's Orations. *The Four vs. Catiline; and others.*

Cicero's Select Letters.

Cornelius Nepos, *complete.*

Horace, *complete.*

Juvenal's Satires, *complete.*

Livy, Books I and II.

Livy, Books XXI and XXII.

Ovid's Metamorphoses, Books I-VII.

Ovid's Metamorphoses, Books VIII-XV.

Plautus' Captivi, and Mostellaria.

Plautus' Trinummus and Menæchmi.

Pliny's Select Letters, *complete in 2 volumes.*

Quintilian, Books X and XII.

Sallust's Catiline, and The Jugurthine War.

Tacitus' Annals, *1st Six Books*

Tacitus' Germany and Agricola.

Terence: Andria, Adelphi, and Phormio.

Virgil's Æneid, *the 1st Six Books.*

Virgil's Eclogues and Georgics.

Æschylus' Prometheus Bound, and Seven Against Thebes.

Aristophanes' Clouds.

Demosthenes On the Crown.

Demosthenes' Olynthiacs and Philippics.

Euripides' Alcestis, and Electra.

Euripides' Iphigenia In Aulis, In Tauris.

Euripides' Medea.

Herodotus, Books VI and VII.

Homer's Iliad, *the 1st Six Books.*

Homer's Odyssey, *1st 12 Books.*

Lysias' Orations.

Plato's Apology, Crito and Phaedo.

Plato's Gorgias.

Sophocles' Œdipus Tyrannus, Electra, and Antigone.

Thucydides, Books I-IV.

Thucydides, Books V-VIII.

Xenophon's Anabasis, *1st 4 Books.*

Xenophon's Hellenica and Symposium (The Banquet).

Xenophon's Memorabilia, *complete.*

Goethe's Egmont.

Goethe's Faust.

Goethe's Iphigenia In Tauris.

Goethe's Hermann and Dorothea.

Lessing's Minna von Barnhelm.

Lessing's Nathan the Wise.

Schiller's Maid of Orleans.

Schiller's Maria Stuart.

Schiller's William Tell.

Feuillet's Romance of a Poor Young

Aristophanes' Birds, and Frogs.   Man.

Others to follow

CPSIA information can be obtained
at www.ICGtesting.com
Printed in the USA
LVHW090615050820
662302LV00009B/301